LOVE : THE TRUE STORY

MR VIVEK KUMAR PANDEY SHAMBHUNATH

ISBN 979-888569509-1

Disclaimer : Disclaimer : During Writing This Book No character & No religious , No Relation Members Are Harmed. It's Only For Study & Entertainment Purpose. Do Not Take Seriously,Written By Mr Vivek Kumar Pandey.

Contents

Foreword

In This Book There is Love Story Given. How Fulfilling The Promise Of Girl etc. During Writing This Book No Character And No Religion Are Harmed. It's Only For Study Purpose. Written By Mr Vivek Kumar Pandey .

Preface

Author biography in English :MY NAME IS VIVEK KUMAR PANDEY . I WAS BORN IN 30 SEP 2002,I AM FROM SURAT GUJARAT INDIA.MY DREAM WAS TO BE GOOD WRITERS ,MY FAMILY SUPPORTED ME TO SUCCESSFUL AND I CAN DO IT MY SELF.How do I write? That is a question, I believe, that can be honestly answered by me."CELEBRATING YOUNGEST WRITER AWARD WINNER IN GUJARAT 1ST RANK" MR PANDEY JI . I may think I did a good job writing something . The reader is the one who decides the quality of my writing. I do find writing to be natural to me and therefore find it to be a real challenge. My trick as a challenged writer is to do the best I can and know that I am happy with the final outcome. It may take a while to do my best and there may be quite a few problems I run into along the way.

I am not a greedy person those who are thinking about me and my self I never tried it anyone people suffering from sadness ,I trying to get promoted people suffering from happiness and joy in your Life Time. Now in current situation in India and also world people are unemployed and have no many but our indian governor help to people to get free food from ration card , i also take part in leadership team ,i am Motivational speaker , Film script writer. There was my two dream firstly writer and secondly actor & also my own film is upcoming soon i done almost completely completed script for my film .I AM GOING TO SAY WORD OF HEART TOUCH OUT PLEASE READ IT" , firstly i thanks my father he supports me in this field they always getting inspired me by own his words and behavior ,they always said that he was a biggest person in the world in future and also they purchase fruit and chocolate for me in anytime & anyway , firstly my father buy him then call me Vivek you want a chocolate i will say yes papa but how many tell me ,papa: you tell me how much i buy him i told 1 or 2 chocolate but my father purchase whole the boxes of chocolate and they get suprised me. MY FATHER WAS BORN IN " 20 SEPTEMBER" 1971 IN INDIA.

1) MY FATHER FAVORITE CLOTHES IS KURTA PAIJMA AND ALSO STYLES SHOE

2) FAVORITE SINGER IS KISHORE DA

3) FAVORITE STATE GUJARAT AND KOLKATA , HIS VILLAGE IN BIHAR

4) FAVORITE COLOR BLACK AND WHITE

THEY ALSO LOVE cricket like IPL and one day t-20 .they also like watching a News daily and heard the song daily ,they also interested in tik tok video but in current time tik tok is banned in india but also few videos are in you tube. In lockdown time my family and me very enjoy day daily. my father play daily ludo with his sister and son, daughter.they always loved tea and coffee anytime call me "। वविेक थोडा़ चाय बनाओना वविेक तुम्हारे हाथ का चाय अच्छा लगता है". I make it tea for my father but some reason after the April to june they are suffering from fever and cough , weakness on 6 June 2020 my father death. they not told me say bye bye his life. After death of 6 June on 10 june my mom and dad anniversary.but my father is Best in the world they can do anything for me please take care of father and respect it of your parents.

CHAPTER ONE

Ch : 1 Fulfilling a Promise

- Ch : 1 Fulfilling a Promise

Ever since the beginning The girl's family member disagree her relationship with the boy. Saying that because of family background, if she insist of being together with the boy, she'll suffer for her whole lifetime.

Because of the pressure applied by family members, she frequently quarrel with him. The girl does love the boy, she used to ask him, "How much do you love me?" Because the boy is not good with words, he used to make her angry. With additional comment from her parents, her mood get even worse. The boy, has become her "anger releasing target". And the boy, just silently allowed her to continuously release her anger on him.

Later, the boy graduated from University. He plan to further study overseas but before he left. He proposed to the girl... " I, don't know how to say nice words but I do know that, I love you. If you agree, I am willing to take care of you, the whole life. About your family members, I will work hard to convince them and agree on us."

"Marry me, will you?", the girl agreed.

And her parents, looking at the effort shown by the boy, agreed with them. Finally, before the boy go oversea, they are engaged. The girl stay back in the hometown, step into the working society where as the boy continuing his study oversea. They maintained their relationship through telephone and letters. Although time is difficult to get through with, but both of them never give up.

One day, the girl left home for work as usual on her way to the bus stop, a car lose control and knock her down. As she awake from unconsciousness, she saw her parents and realize how seriously she got hurt and how fortunate of her, not to get killed.

Looking at her parents, with their faced got all wet by their tears, she tried to comfort them. But then, she found out that She can't even spell out a word, she tried her best to make some voice but all she managed, was to breath without any voice. She's mute. According to the doctor, the injury affected her brain, and that cause her to be mute for the rest of her life. Listening to her parents persuade, but can't even reply with a single word, the girl collapsed. Throughout the days, others than crying silently, still it is crying.

Later, the girl discharged from hospital. Returning to her home, everything is still like before. Except that the phone ring, has turned into the worst nightmare of hers. Ring after ring, continuously stimulate her, stimulating her pain But she can't tell the boy. She don't want to be a burden to him, and wrote him a letter telling him that she no longer want to wait, the relationship between them ended, and even returned him the engagement ring. Facing the letters and telephone from the boy, all she can do, is to allow tears falling from her eyes.

Her father decided to move, after seeing the pain she is suffering. Hoping that she could forget everything and be happier into a new environment, the girl started to learn, slowly picking up sign language and start over again. Also telling herself to forget the boy.

One day, her best friend tell her that the boy's back. He's searching all around for her, she asked her best friend not to tell him about her and asked her to tell him to forget her. After that for more than a year there was no news of boy. One day her best friend tells her, that the boy is getting married soon, and passed the Wedding Card to her. She open the card sadly, but she found her name on the card.

The moment she want to ask her best friend, the boy appear in front of her. With an unfamiliar sign language, he told her "I spent more than a year's time, to force myself to learn sign language, in order to tell you, I have not forgot our promise, give me an opportunity, let me be your voice. I love you."Looking at the slow sign language by the boy, and the engagement ring she gave back to him, She finally smiled.

- Moral: Do not be a coward and run away whenever there is a problem, remember that every problem has a solution, never ever break someone's heart, you may not know when it will happen to you.

CHAPTER TWO

Ch : 2 Having a Best Friend

- Ch : 2 Having a Best Friend

A story tells that two friends were walking through the desert. During some point of the journey they had an argument, and one friend slapped the other one in the face.

The one who got slapped was hurt, but without saying anything, wrote in the sand "Today my best friend slapped me in the face".

They kept on walking until they found an oasis, where they decided to take a bath. The one who had been slapped got stuck in the mire and started drowning, but the friend saved him. After he recovered from the near drowning, he wrote on a stone "Today my best friend saved my life".

The friend who had slapped and saved his best friend asked him, "After I hurt you, you wrote in the sand and now, you write on a stone, why?" The other friend replied "When someone hurts us we should write it down in sand where winds of forgiveness can erase it away. But, when someone does something good for us, we must engrave it in stone where no wind can ever erase it."

- Moral: Do not value the things you have in your life. But value who you have in your life.

CHAPTER THREE

Ch : 3 Story of Regret

- Ch : 3 Story of Regret

There was this guy who believed very much in true love and decided to take his time to wait for his right girl to appear. He believed that there would definitely be someone special out there for him, but none came. Every year at Christmas, his ex-girlfriend would return from Vancouver to look him up. He was aware that she still held some hope of re-kindling the past romance with him. He did not wish to mislead her in any way. So he would always get one of his girl friends to pose as his steady whenever she came back. That went on for several years and each year, the guy would get a different girl to pose as his romantic interest.

So whenever the ex-girlfriend came to visit him, she would be led into believing that it was all over between her and the guy. The girl took all those rather well, often trying to casually tease him about his different girlfriends, or so, as it seemed! In fact, the girl often wept in secret whenever she saw him with another girl, but she was too proud to admit it. Still, every Christmas, she returned, hoping to re-kindle some form of romance. But each time, she returned to Vancouver feeling disappointed.

Finally she decided that she could not play that game any longer. Therefore, she confronted him and professed that after all those years, he was still the only man that she had ever loved.

Although the guy knew of her feelings for him, he was still taken back and have never expected her to react that way. He always thought that she would slowly forget about him over time and come to terms that it was all over between them. Although he was touched by her undying love for him and wanted so much to accept her again, he remembered why he rejected her in the first place-she was not the one he wanted.

So he hardened his heart and turned her down cruelly. Since then, three years have passed and the girl never return anymore. They never even wrote to each other. The guy went on with his life... still searching for the one but somehow deep inside him, he missed the girl.

On the Christmas of 1995, he went to his friend's party alone. Hey, how come all alone this year? Where are all your girlfriends? What happened to that Vancouver babe who joins you every Christmas?, asked one of his friend. He felt warm and comforted by his friend's queries about her, still he just surged on.

Then, he came upon one of his many girlfriends whom he once requested to pose as his steady. He wanted so much to ignore her ..... not that he was impolite, but because at that moment, he just didn't feel comfortable with those girlfriends anymore. It was almost like he was being judged by them. The girl saw him and shouted across the floor for him. Unable to avoid her, he went up to acknowledge her.

Hi... how are you? Enjoying the party? the girl asked.

Sure... yeah!, he replied.

She was slightly tipsy... must be from the whiskey on her hand. She continued, Why...? Don't you need someone to pose as your girlfriend this year? Then he answered, No, there is no need for that anymore...

Before he can continue, he was interrupted, Oh yes! Must have found a girlfriend! You haven't been searching for one for the past years, right? The man looked up, as if he has struck gold, his face beamed and looked directly at the drunken girl. He replied, Yes... you are right! I haven't been looking for anyone for the past years.

With that, the man darted across the floor and out the door, leaving the lady in much bewilderment. He finally realized that he has already found his dream girl, and she was... the Vancouver girl all along! The drunken lady has said something that awoken him.

All along he has found his girl. That was why he did not bother to look further when he realized she was not coming back. It was not any specific girl he was seeking! It was perfection that he wanted, and yes... perfection! Relationship is something both parties should work on. Realizing that he had let away someone so important in his life, he decided to call her immediately. His whole mind was flooded with fear. He was afraid that she might have found someone new or no longer had the same feelings anymore... For once, he felt the fear of losing someone.

As it was Christmas eve, the line was quite hard to get through, especially an overseas call. He tried again and again, never giving up. Finally, he got through.... precisely at 1200 midnight. He confessed his love for her and the girl was moved to tears. It seemed that she never got over him! Even after so long, she was still waiting for him, never giving up.

He was so excited to meet her and to begin his new chapter of their lives. He decided to fly to Vancouver to join her. It was the happiest time of their lives! But their happy time was short-lived. Two days before he was supposed to fly to Vancouver, he received a call from her father. She had a head-on car collision with a drunken driver. She passed away after 6 hours in a coma.

The guy was devastated, as it was a complete loss. Why did fate played such cruel games with him? He cursed the heaven for taking her away from him, denying even one last look at her! How cruel he cursed! How he damned the Gods...!! How he hated himself... for taking so long to realize his mistake!! That was in 1996.

- Moral: Treasure what you have... Time is too slow for those who wait, Too swift for those who fear, Too long for those who grief, Too short for those who rejoice, But for those who love... Time is Eternity. For all you out there with someone special in your heart, cherish that person, cherish every moment that you spend together that special someone, for in life, anything can happen anytime. You may painfully regret, only to realize that it is too late.

CHAPTER FOUR

Ch : 4 Who or What do we love more?

- Ch : 4 Who or What do we love more?

A man was polishing his new car; his 4 yr old daughter picked up a stone and scratched on the side of the car. In anger, the furious Man took his child's hand hit it many times, not realizing he was using a wrench. At the hospital, the child lost all his fingers due to multiple fractures.

When the child saw her father, with painful eyes he asked 'Dad when will my fingers grow back?' The man was so hurt and speechless. He went back to the car and kicked it many times. Devastated by his own actions, sitting in front of the car he looked at the scratches, His daughter had written 'LOVE YOU DAD'.

- Moral: Remember, Anger and Love have no limit. Always remember that "Things are to be used and people are to be loved". But the problem in today's world is that "People are being used Things are being loved".

CHAPTER FIVE

Ch : 5 Why Should I feel Bad

- Ch : 5 Why Should I feel Bad

Once, there was this guy, who was in love with a girl. She wasn't the most beautiful and gorgeous but for him, she was everything. He used to dream about her, about spending the rest of life with her. His friends told him, "why do you dream so much about her, when you don't even know if she loves you or not? First tell her your feelings, and get to know if she likes you or not".

He felt that was the right way. The girl knew from the beginning, that this guy loves her. One day when he proposed, she rejected him. His friends thought he would take alcohol, drugs etc and ruin his life. To their surprise, he was not depressed.

When they asked him how was it that he is not sad, he replied, "'why should I feel bad? I lost one who never loved me and she lost the one who really loved and cared for her."

- Moral: True Love is Hard to Get. Love is all about giving to other person without greed of gaining anything in return, if other person rejects it, its him/her who will be losing the most important thing in life. So never feel dejected.

CHAPTER SIX

Ch : 6 Old Man Love for his Wife

- Ch : 6 Old Man Love for his Wife

Once in morning came an elderly gentleman in hospital. He came to get his stitches removed from his thumb.A nurse came to attend him. Nurse checked his vitals and told him to wait as it would be over an hour before doctor would be able to see him. While attending old man nurse noticed that he seemed to be in hurry.

So nurse told him to wait but old man asked him to hurry if possible. Seeing this nurse thought that she would evaluate his wounds and if possible would take care of it instead of making him wait.

On examining nurse found that wounds were healed, so nurse went to get supplies and came back to old man and started redressing his wound.

As they started talking nurse asked him, "Do you have any doctor's appointment as you seem to be in hurry..?"

Old man replied, "No, i need to go to nursing home to eat breakfast with my wife."

Nurse then asked about his wife and came to know that she had been living in nursing home for while and was suffering from Alzheimer's disease.

As nurse finished dressing she said, "Would she worry if you get there a bit late??"Old man replied, "No.. She no longer remember who i am and had not recognized him in last five years.."

Nurse was surprised and said, "She doesn't recognize you yet you go to have breakfast with her every morning?? Why??" .Old man smiled and replied, "She doesn't know me but i still know who she is.."

- Moral:

For Person in Love time, place or health nothing matter. What matter's is love and care for his/her Partner despite facing any kind of difficulties.

CHAPTER SEVEN

Ch : 7 Lesson for Every Son

- Ch : 7 Lesson for Every Son

One evening, a son took his father to a restaurant. After getting seated there. Son called waiter and ordered food.Father was old and weak because of this while eating food, his father dropped food on his short and trousers.

While son was calming having food with father, other diners sitting there looked at them with disgust. Every one sitting there were watching them with disgust, as father was not able to eat properly and dropping food. Even when all the diners were staring at them still son didn't seem to be embarrassed by all this.

After they finished eating, son quietly took his father to wash room, wiped the food dropped on his shirt and trousers, combed his hairs and fitted his spectacles firmly.

When they came out of washroom, all diners sitting there watched them in dead silence and were not able to grasp how someone could embarrass themselves publicly like that..!!

Son payed bill and started to walk out of restaurant with his father.

At that time, one of the old man among-st diners called out to young man and said, "Don't you think you have left behind something??"

Young man replied, "No sir, i haven't.."

Old ma retorted, "Yes you have...!! You have left a lesson for every son and hope for every father.."

- Moral:

When we are small and did silly things in public, our parents never feel embarrass about it then why don't children take their old parents out in public and spend time with them without feeling embarrassed??

Always Love and Care for Your Parents When they Get Old. We should Learn to Respect and Care for parents When they need it most. Never Make them feel Unwanted Because they are the one Who Always love us Unconditionally all their Life Even when we Make Mistakes.

CHAPTER EIGHT

Ch : 8 Scars in Your Life

- Ch : 8 Scars in Your Life

On a hot summer day, A little boy and his mother were inside a lake house. Little boy decided to go for a swim in lake behind his house. Boy was really excited to go into lake and swim in cool lake so he just ran out.

Boy went into lake and swam far without realizing that he swan right into middle of that lake. Boy's mother looked out of window and saw an alligator approaching toward his son.

As she saw both of them getting closer to each other, she ran toward little boy and yelled as loud as she could. She shouted about alligator approaching him and asked him to swim back toward house.

Hearing voice of his mother, boy got alarmed and made U-turn to swim towards his mother but it was too late. Just as mother reached her little boy and grabbed his arm, at same moment alligator snatched on his legs.

That began a tug war between two. Alligator was too strong but mother was too passionate to let her son go.

At same time, a farmer happen to pass by and heard scream of little boy and his mother. Farmer raced toward lake and took his aim at alligator and shot him.

Remarkable, after getting treated for weeks in hospital boy survived.

A newspaper reporter came to interview boy after incident and asked him about the incident. Boy lifted his pants from legs which was extremely scarred by the vicious attack of animal.

But then, with pride he said to reporters, "Look at my arms. I have great scars on my arms too."

Newspaper reporter, "Why these scars are great??"

Boy replied, "I have these scars on arm because my mom wouldn't let go.."

• Moral:

Similarly in our Life we have Scars from painful past. Sometimes, we foolishly made into difficult situations and we forget that enemy is waiting.

That's when Tug of war begin Between Life and God. That's why Some wounds we have because God wouldn't let go. We should be very Grateful to God for being there with us.

CHAPTER NINE

Ch : 9 Brother's Love

- Ch : 9 Brother's Love

In hospital, there was little girl who was suffering from a very rare and serious disease. She had little brother who was just 5 years old.

Her brother himself was suffering from same disease and miraculously he survived and had developed antibodies to combat that illness.Doctors found that girls only chance of recovery is blood transfusion from her 5 years old brother.

Doctors knew it will be a long process and boy had to go through medical process for transfusion so they decided to ask him first and make him comfortable before going ahead with transfusion.So a doctor went to little kid and asked him, "If you give your blood to your sister then she will be healthy again. Are you willing to give your blood to your sister??"

Kid hesitated for a while and then said, "Yes, I will do it. If it will save her.."After the transfusion process started, boy was lying next to her sister's bed smiling. slowly his smile faded and he looked up to doctor and asked in trembling voice, "Will i die right away??"

Boy misunderstood doctors when they asked him about giving blood to his sister.

Doctor looked at innocent boy and thought to himself, "Boy thought that he had to give all the blood to her sister and after that he will die and yet he agreed to give blood to her and gave up his life for her."

Doctor went to boy and cleared what he had misunderstood.

CHAPTER TEN

Ch : 10 Young Girl Love for Prince

- Ch : 10 Young Girl Love for Prince

In ancient china, It was tradition that if prince has to be married before he can become crowned emperor. There was a prince who was about to be crowned. So he needed to find a young woman whom he could trust and get married to.

Once there was a who had to be crowned in few days so Prince decided to summon all the young women from his kingdom in order to find most worthy candidate.

There was an old lady who used to serve at palace. When heard the news she got sad because she knew her daughter nurtured a secret love for prince. After getting home she told her daughter about it. Her daughter decided that she would go to palace. Old lady got worried after knowing her decision.

Old lady said to her daughter, "What will you do there?? There will be all beautiful and rich girls from kingdom will be present there.."

Daughter replied, "Mother I know i won't be chosen but it's my only chance to spend time with prince and that makes me happy. I will go to palace tomorrow."

Next day when young girl reached palace, she saw young women from all around kingdom were present there wearing beautiful cloths and jewelry, prepared to do anything to seize this opportunity to marry prince.

In presence of all members of court and girls prince announced a challenge.

He said, "I will give you each a seed. After six months time, young woman who brings me the loveliest flower will be my wife and future empress."All girls took seed and left. Poor young girl also took her seed and planted it in a pot. She nurtured and took care of it with love. She believed that her love is true and flower will grow as large as her love for prince.

Girl saw that no shoot appeared even after three months have passed and nothing had grown in her pot. Young girl consulted farmers, peasants but nothing happened. With each days he felt that her dream have moved father away.

At last six months were over and still nothing had grown in that pot. She knew she had no flower to show still she decided to go back to palace with that pot. She reached palace on final day.

On final day all court member and girls arrived. She saw that all other candidates had wonderful results and each one had lovely flower, she was the only one holding a flowerless pot.

Finally, prince entered courtroom and inspected all candidates pot and announced result. He chose Servant's daughter poor young girl as his would be wife.

All other girls present there got angry and protested that she had nothing in her pot and prince had chosen someone who had not managed to grow anything at all.

Prince calmed them down and explained the reason.

Prince said, "This young woman was the only one who cultivated the flower that made her worthy of becoming the empress: the flower of honesty. All the seeds I handed out were sterile and nothing could ever have grown from them."

- Moral:

We should not feel Disappointed if Things doesn't go Way we think it should be. We should have Confidence and Stay Honesty and True because Honesty is best Policy.

CHAPTER ELEVEN

Ch : 11 Losing Everything in Moment of Anger

- Ch : 11 Losing Everything in Moment of Anger

A couple had been married for 10 years but they didn't had any child. They stayed with each other and really hoped that they will have a child before their 11th anniversary. Their family and friends were pursuing them to get a divorce but they didn't wanted to get separated because of strong love between them.

Months passed.

One day while husband was returning home from work, he saw his wife walking down street with a man. They were looking very happy. After a week again husband saw his wife with same man again. Husband saw them many times roaming places with each other. Hugging each other.

One evening while husband was returning home, He saw that man dropped her off with a good bye kiss on her cheek. Husband got angry and sad.

After a hectic day at work, Husband was home. While he was holding a glass jug to get water, Phone rang. He received the call. As soon as he picked the call voice came form other side saying, "Hello dear, I will be coming to your home this evening to see you as i promise, I hope.."

Husband hung up call before hearing any further. Husband thought to himself, "It was male voice and i am sure it's same person i have seen with my wife many times." He thought he had lost his wife to another man and thinking that glass jug fell from his hand and shattered into pieces.

Listening to noise, his wife came running to him and asked, "Is everything okay??"

In anger he pushed his wife. She fell and wasn't moving. Few seconds later husband realized that she fell on the broken jug pieces and a large piece has pierced her. Husband tried to feel her breath, heartbeat but there wasn't any.

His wife was dead. He saw an envelope in her hand. He took it and read it. He was shocked by what was written in it.

It reads :

"My loving husband, words can't express how i feel so... I had to write down this letter. I have been seeing a doctor for over a week and i wanted to be sure before giving you the big news.

Doctor have confirmed that i am pregnant. Our baby is due 5 months from now. Doctor i have been seeing is my long lost brother whom i contacted after our marriage. He promised me to take care of me and baby and will give us best care without any fee.

He promised to have dinner with us tonight. I had to write to you because i am so happy. Thanks for staying by my side.

Your loving wife."

Letter fell from his hands. At same time he heard knock on the door it was same man he had seen with his wife. He came in and said, "Hello, i am John, your wife's brother......." Suddenly he notice his sister lying in pool of her blood. He rushed her to hospital where she was confirmed dead.

- Moral:

We should not be Quick to Judge Other person. In Relationships we should Try to talk and clear things. We should not let our Anger control us because Not everything we see or hear is true.!

CHAPTER TWELVE

Ch : 12 Arrogant Rich Girl Story

- Ch : 12 Arrogant Rich Girl Story

Once a poor boy fell in love with a rich man daughter. Boy loved her a lot so one day he proposed to her.

Girl rejected him by saying, "Listen, your monthly salary is even less than my daily expenses. How can i live with you? How could you even thought of coming to me and ask me?? I can never ever love you. Forget about me and go find someone of your level to get engaged."

Even after knowing girl's thought he still loved her and after getting rejected boy left but couldn't forget her.

10 years later they stumbled into each other in a shopping mall.

Girl recognized him and said, "Hey!! You.. how are you?? I am married now He is very smart and do you know how much my husband's salary..!! it's 20,000$ per month. Can you beat that??

Boy eye's got wet hearing those words from same person. A few seconds later her husband came around.

Before girl could say a word seeing the guy her husband said, "Sir, you are here! you have met my wife."

"This is my boss. I am one those working for his 100 million $ project." husband said looking at his wife.

Husband continued, "He is very good person and do you know my dear, My boss loved a girl but he couldn't win her heart that's why he remained unmarried. How lucky would that girl have been, if she married my boss now..!! Now days who would have loved someone so much."

Girl got totally shocked but couldn't say a word after that.

- Moral:

Life is too short so don't be too arrogant and proud of yourself and look down on others current situation. Things change time change. Don't under estimate anyone because everyone can have a great future.

CHAPTER THIRTEEN

Ch : 13 Boy and Girl After Marriage

- Ch : 13 Boy and Girl After Marriage

A boy and girl loved each other very much. One day boy proposed girl. Girl asked, "What am I to you?"

Boy thought for a moment and then looked into her eyes and said, "You are missing part of my heart."

Girl smiled and accepted his proposal. Soon they both got married and lived a happy life for a while. With time young couple began to drift apart because of their busy schedule. Due to daily worries and work their life became difficult.

With each passing day couple started to have quarrels and with this their relation got affected badly with time it became worse.One day after fight girl ran out of the house and shouted to her husband, "You don't love me."

Boy hated her silliness and out of impulse said, "May it was a mistake. You were never the missing part of my life!!"

Suddenly girl turned quiet and she knew spoken words can't be taken back. With tears in her eyes she went home, pack her things and before leaving him left a note for him.

Note said, "May be I was never missing part of your life, let me go and search for some who is.... Lets go our separate ways. This way it would be less painful."

Five year passed..

Boy never married again but he used to keep information about girl somehow. He knew that she had left country and was living her dreams. He used to regret about what happened but never went to girl and tried to patch up. He never wanted to accept the fact that he missed her and still missing her in his life.

One day at the airport while he was going away on business trip he saw her. She was standing alone just few steps away. She saw him and smiled at him gently.

Boy asked, "How are you?"

Girl replied, "I am fine how about you? did you find love of your life?"

Boy answered, "No.."

Girl said, "I will be flying in next flight."

Boy said, "I will be back in 2 week. Give me a call then.."

Girl smiled and waved goodbye to him.

Same evening boy heard of plane crash. Same plane on which girl went. Boy tried to found about her and he got to know that she was dead. Once again like before he felt pain of missing her. he finally knew that she was the missing part that he had broken carelessly and now she was gone forever.

- Moral:

Sometimes people say things out of anger but we should not act in impulse and try to think wisely and give time because a moment of anger could result in lifetime of punishment.

CHAPTER FOURTEEN

Ch : 14 Heart Touching Love Story

- Ch : 14 Heart Touching Love Story

It's story of a Boy and Girl. They were best friend for years and used to talk on phone for hours and text each other whole day. There wouldn't be a day on which they didn't contact and talk to each other. Everything was great. They used to be happy in each other company and enjoy.

But one day boy didn't call of replied to girl for a day. Girl got worried and knew something was wrong. At night in her room she was crying and at that time she realized that how much he meant to her.

Next day in morning she got a call. It was from boy.

Boy: Hi

Girl: I am so glad that you called, What happened to you yesterday?

Boy: i was busy.

(After silence for min)

Boy: I think we should stop talking.

Girl: What? but why?

Boy: Sorry. Bye.

After this boy disconnected call. Girl was shocked. She couldn't understand anything and was feeling lonely, rejected and broken. After thinking she decided to make a last try to get him back. So, She called him.

Girl: Hi

Boy: Why are you calling me?

Girl: I need to ask u something.

Boy: Go ahead

Girl (With heavy heart): Are you alright?

She tried to talk but she thought may be he really doesn't care. She broke off and left her house leaving a note.

Few hours later boy got a call. It was to inform him that girl got hit by a car and her condition was serious. Boy rushed to hospital and went to see her. He was sitting beside her holding her hand.

Boy: I am sorry it's all my fault But.. i promise i will make it up to u.

Girl: I am not gonna get better!!

Boy: Don't say that.

Girl: Just tell me one thing why you asked me to leave?

To this question of her boy tell her the truth that he has heart problem and he didn't wanted her to get worried because there was risk that he would die.

Boy continued ans said, "I did this because I Love You...!!"

I Love u Too.. Girl said and her heart stop beating. Just after 10 mins boy also died because of heart attack. As he could live with the thought that she died because of him.

• Moral:

If you Love someone then Don't hold back your Feelings. Never hide your problems and feeling from the one who cares for you and Love you.

CHAPTER FIFTEEN

Ch : 15 Story of Boy and Girl Who Loved But

Ch : 15 Story of Boy and Girl Who Loved But
It's story of girl and boy who loved but..!!

- 10th Grade:-

As I sat there in English class, I stared at the girl next to me. She was my 'best friend'. I stared at her long, silky hair, and wished she was mine. But she didn't notice me like that, and I knew it. After class, she walked up to me and asked me for the notes. I handed them to her.

She Thanked me and gave a Kiss on my Cheek. All I wanted to do is to tell her how I feel about her. I lover her and wanted to tell her that I want her to be mine but I was too shy to tell her.

- 11th grade:-

The phone rang. On the other end, it was her. She was in tears, mumbling on and on about how her love had broke her heart. She asked me to come over because she didn't want to be alone, So I did. As I sat next to her on the sofa, I stared at her soft eyes, wishing she was mine. After 2 hours, one Drew Barrymore movie, and three bags of chips, she decided to go home.

She Thanked me and gave a Kiss on my Cheek. All I wanted to do is to tell her how I feel about her. I lover her and wanted to tell her that I want her to be mine but I was too shy to tell her.

- Senior year:-

One fine day she walked to my locker. "My date is sick" she said, "hes not gonna go" well, I didn't have a date, and in 7ᵗʰ grade, we made a promise that if neither of us had dates, we would go together just as 'best friends'. So we did. That night, after everything was over, I was standing at her front door step. I stared at her as She smiled at me and stared at me with her crystal eyes.

She Thanked me and gave a Kiss on my Cheek. All I wanted to do is to tell her how I feel about her. I lover her and wanted to tell her that I want her to be mine but I was too shy to tell her.

• Graduation:-

A day passed, then a week, then a month. Before I could blink, it was graduation day. I watched as her perfect body floated like an angel up on stage to get her diploma. I wanted her to be mine-but she didn't notice me like that, and I knew it. Before everyone went home, she came to me in her smock and hat, and cried as I hugged her.

She said, "you are my Best friend." and gave a Kiss on my Cheek. All I wanted to do is to tell her how I feel about her. I lover her and wanted to tell her that I want her to be mine but I was too shy to tell her.

• Marriage:-

Now I sit in church. That girl is getting married now. and drive off to her new life, married to another man. I wanted her to be mine, but she didn't see me like that, and I knew it. But before she drove away, she came to me and said 'you came !'.

She Thanked me and gave a Kiss on my Cheek. All I wanted to do is to tell her how I feel about her. I lover her and wanted to tell her that I want her to be mine but I was too shy to tell her.

• Death:-

Years passed, I looked down at the coffin of a girl who used to be my 'best friend'.

At the service, they read a diary entry she had wrote in her high school years.

- This is what it read:

"I stare at him wishing he was mine, but he doesn't notice me like that, and I know it. I want to tell him, I want him to know that I don't want to be just friends,
I love him but I'm just too shy, and I don't know why. I wish he would tell me he loved me!"
"I wish I did too" I thought to my self, and I cried!!

- Moral:

If you love someone, Tell Them, Don't let your heart be broken by words left unspoken.

CHAPTER SIXTEEN

Ch : 16 Heart Touching Poor Husband Wife Story

- Ch : 16 Heart Touching Poor Husband Wife Story

One day Wife asked Husband to buy her comb so that she can grow her hair well and to be well groomed.

Her husband couldn't afford to buy her comb and felt sorry. He refused her and explained that he didn't even have enough money to fix strap of his watch. After knowing this she didn't insist on her request.

Next day, as Husband was going for work, he passed by watch shop and went inside to sold his damaged watch so that he can buy comb his wife.

In evening he came home with comb for his wife and he was very happy to give this to his wife so that she can take better care of her long hairs. But to his surprise he saw that his wife hair were cut short. When he asked why she got her hairs got cut short?

She replied with a Smile, "I sold my hair and here is new strap for your watch."

Tears came out from their eyes, not for futility of their actions but for the love they had for each other.

- Moral:

To Love is Something and to be Loved is Something but to Love and To be Loved in return is Everything. So never take Love for ranted and always Value the Ones who Love you.

CHAPTER SEVENTEEN

Ch : 17 Father Love for Daughter

- Ch : 17 Father Love for Daughter

One day Little 12 years old girl asked her Father, "What are you going to gift me for my next birthday?"

Father Smiled and said, "There is much time, so wait till your Birthday."

Just after few days of this conversation, the girl fainted and was rushed to the Hospital. After checking on girl, Doctor came out and informed family that girl had a Bad Heart and probably she will die. Everyone in family was shocked to hear that and didn't knew what to do.

While girl was lying on bed in hospital and her father was sitting near her. She asked, "Daddy, Am I gona die?"

Father replied, "No dear, You will live." He gave her a warm hug and kissed her on forehead and left weeping.

Girl said, "How can you be so sure daddy?"

Father turned around and replied, "I Know."

After some time Girl got treated and was recovering, at same time she turned 13. After she came home, she found a Letter on her bed.

It says: "My Sweet Kid, If you are reading this, It means everything went well as I told you. You remember? Once you asked me what am I gonna Gift you for your Birthday. Well, at that time i didn't knew What I am gonna give you but Now my Present to you is MY HEART"

Father donated his heart for her daughter..!!

- Moral:

Our Parents Loves us, make selfless sacrifices to keep up happy and safe. So, always respect and Love your Parents because you don't know what they had given up for you.

CHAPTER EIGHTEEN

Ch : 18 Life Changing Event at Airport

- Ch : 18 Life Changing Event at Airport

Story of man who experienced a life changing event at airport while he was waiting there to pick up his friend. As the man was trying to locate his friends at airport, He noticed a man coming toward him carrying his bags and stopped right next to him.

After reaching his family he first motioned to his younger son (6yrs old) and they gave each other a long and loving hug. As the separated father said to his son, "It's so good to see you son. I missed you so much." His son replied softly, "Me too Dad."

Now the man stoop up to his elder son (10yrs old) and holding his son's face in his hands with love he said, "I love you so much Zach." And the too hugged lovingly.

While all this was happening, Man saw a baby girl (1yr old) excitedly in her mother's arm, never taking eyes off his returning father. While the man gently took his baby girl from his wife he said ,"Hi baby girl." And kissed her all over and held her close to his chest. The little girl instantly got relaxed and laid on her father's shoulder.

After having some moments with his daughter, he handed little girl to the oldest son and said, "I have saved best for last." and proceeded to give his wife most passionate kiss and silently said, "I Love You So Much..!!" While holding each others hand they gave each other big smiles.

For an instant it seemed liked they were like newly married couple but looking at their children Man knew that it couldn't be possible.

Man waiting for his friend suddenly felt uncomfortable but couldn't resist himself from asking, "Wow! How long you two have been married?"

He replied, "Been together for 14 years and married for 12 of those."

Now, out of curiosity man asked, "How long you have been away?"

"Two whole days!", Man replied still beaming with his joyous smile.

Man was stunned to her "Two days!!" as Looking at the intensity of greeting. He already assumed that person had been gone for weeks at least if not months.

Amazed by the love and affection of couple even after so many years man mumbled to himself, "I hope my marriage is still that passionate after 12 years."

The man who just met his family suddenly stopped smiling and look into eyes of man and told him something. He said, "Don't hope my Friend… Decide." and shook hands with him saying, "God Bless!"

CHAPTER NINETEEN

Ch : 19 Blind Girl Story

- Ch : 19 Blind Girl Story

There was a girl who hated herself just because she was blind. She used to hate everyone around her except her Boyfriend. He was always there for her even after the accident in which she got blind and her behavior changed towards life.

She always used to say that if she could see the world. She would marry her boyfriend. One day, someone donated a pair of eyes to her.

She had an operation and now she could see everything, everyone including her boyfriend and was very happy.

Seeing her happy boyfriend was happy too and asked her, "Now that you can see the world, will you marry me?"

But the girl was shocked to see that her boyfriend was blind too. So, she refuse to marry him.

This left her boyfriend heart broken and he walked away with tears in this eyes and left a note to her saying, "JUST TAKE CARE OF MY EYES DEAR."

CHAPTER TWENTY

Ch : 20 Husband And Wife Sad Story

- Ch : 20 Husband And Wife Sad Story

When I got home that night as my wife served dinner, I held her hand and said, I've got something to tell you. She sat down and ate quietly. Again I observed the hurt in her eyes. Suddenly I didn't know how to open my mouth. But I had to let her know what I was thinking. I want a divorce. I raised the topic calmly.

She didn't seem to be annoyed by my words, instead she asked me softly, why? I avoided her question. This made her angry. She threw away the chopsticks and shouted at me, you are not a man! That night, we didn't talk to each other. She was weeping. I knew she wanted to find out what had happened to our marriage. But I could hardly give her a satisfactory answer; she had lost my heart to Jane. I didn't love her anymore. I just pitied her!

With a deep sense of guilt, I drafted a divorce agreement which stated that she could own our house, our car, and 30% stake of my company. She glanced at it and then tore it into pieces. The woman who had spent ten years of her life with me had become a stranger. I felt sorry for her wasted time, resources and energy but I could not take back what I had said for I loved Jane so dearly. Finally she cried loudly in front of me, which was what I had expected to see. To me her cry was actually a kind of release. The idea of divorce which had obsessed me for several weeks seemed to be firmer and clearer now.

The next day, I came back home very late and found her writing something at the table. I didn't have supper but went straight to sleep and fell asleep very fast because I was tired after an eventful day with Jane.

When I woke up, she was still there at the table writing. I just did not care so I turned over and was asleep again.

In the morning she presented her divorce conditions. She didn't want anything from me, but needed a month's notice before the divorce. She requested that in that one month, we both try to live as normal a life as possible. Her reason for this conditions were simple. Our son had his exams in a month's time and she didn't want to disrupt him with our broken marriage.

This was agreeable to me. But she had something more, she asked me to recall how I had carried her into out bridal room on our wedding day. She requested that every day for the month's duration I carry her out of our bedroom to the front door ever morning. I thought she was going crazy. Just to make our last days together bearable I accepted her odd request.

I told Jane about my wife's divorce conditions. She laughed loudly and thought it was absurd. No matter what tricks she applies, she has to face the divorce, she said scornfully.

My wife and I hadn't had any body contact since my divorce intention was explicitly expressed. So when I carried her out on the first day, we both appeared clumsy. Our son clapped behind us, daddy is holding mommy in his arms. His words brought me a sense of pain. From the bedroom to the sitting room, then to the door, I walked over ten meters with her in my arms. She closed her eyes and said softly; don't tell our son about the divorce. I nodded, feeling somewhat upset. I put her down outside the door. She went to wait for the bus to work. I drove alone to the office.

On the second day, both of us acted much more easily. She leaned on my chest. I could smell the fragrance of her blouse. I realized that I hadn't looked at this woman carefully for a long time. I realized she was not young any more. There were fine wrinkles on her face, her hair was graying! Our marriage had taken its toll on her. For a minute I wondered what I had done to her.

On the fourth day, when I lifted her up, I felt a sense of intimacy returning. This was the woman who had given ten years of her life to me.

On the fifth and sixth day, I realized that our sense of intimacy was growing again. I didn't tell Jane about this. It became easier to carry her as the month slipped by. Perhaps the everyday workout made me stronger.

She was choosing what to wear one morning. She tried on quite a few dresses but could not find a suitable one. Then she sighed, all my dresses have grown bigger. I suddenly realized that she had grown so thin, that was the reason why I could carry her more easily. Suddenly it hit me. She had buried so much pain and bitterness in her heart. Subconsciously I reached out and touched her head.

Our son came in at the moment and said, Dad, it's time to carry mom out. To him, seeing his father carrying his mother out had become an essential part of his life. My wife gestured to our son to come closer and hugged him tightly. I turned my face away because I was afraid I might change my mind at this last-minute. I then held her in my arms, walking from the bedroom, through the sitting room, to the hallway. Her hand surrounded my neck softly and naturally. I held her body tightly, it was just like our wedding day.

But her much lighter weight made me sad. On the last day, when I held her in my arms I could hardly move a step. Our son had gone to school. I held her tightly and said, I hadn't noticed that our life lacked intimacy. I drove to office and jumped out of the car swiftly without locking the door. I was afraid any delay would make me change my mind. I walked upstairs. Jane opened the door and I said to her, Sorry, Jane, I do not want the divorce anymore.

She looked at me, astonished, and then touched my forehead. Do you have a fever? She said. I moved her hand off my head. Sorry, Jane, I said, I won't divorce. My marriage life was boring probably because she and I didn't value the details of our lives, not because we didn't love each other anymore. Now I realize that since I carried her into my home on our wedding day I am supposed to hold her until death do us apart.

Jane seemed to suddenly wake up. She gave me a loud slap and then slammed the door and burst into tears. I walked downstairs and drove away. At the floral shop on the way, I ordered a bouquet of flowers for my wife. The sales girl asked me what to write on the card. I smiled and wrote, "I'll carry you out every morning until death do us apart".

That evening I arrived home, flowers in my hands, a smile on my face, I run up stairs, only to find my wife in the bed – dead.

My wife had been fighting cancer for months and I was so busy with Jane to even notice. She knew that she would die soon and she wanted to save me from the whatever negative reaction from our son, in case we push through with the divorce. At least, in the eyes of our son— I'm a loving husband.

• Moral:

The small details of your lives are what really matter in a relationship. So find time to be your spouse's friend and do those little things for each other.

CHAPTER TWENTY-ONE

Ch : 21 An Island Where Feelings Lived

- Ch : 21 An Island Where Feelings Lived

Once there was a island where all feelings lived: Happiness, Sadness, Knowledge, including Love. One day they got to know that the island was going to sank, So all constructed boats and left except Love. Love was the only one who stayed because it wanted to hold out until the last moment.

When the island almost sank Love decided to ask for help.

Richness was passing by in grand boat. Love saw and asked "Richness, can you take me with you?"

Richness Replied, "There is no place for you as i already have lots of gold and silver to take with me."

The love saw vanity passing by and asked, "Please help me."

Vanity answered, "I can't help you as you are all wet and might damage my boat."

Now love saw sadness and asked it, "Take me with you."

Sadness refused saying, "Love I am already so sad that i need to be with myself only.

Similarly all other feelings passed by and all refused to take love with them.

Suddenly Love heard a voice, "Come Love, I will take you." It was an elder (Knowledge). When they arrived at a dry land, after leaving Love elder went away. Realizing how much he owed elder, Love asked him, "Who helped me?"

"It was Time." Elder replied.

Love asked again, "Why did Time helped me?" Knowledge smiled with deep Wisdom and answered, "Because only Time is capable of understanding how valuable Love is."

- Moral:

We can understand the Value of love only with Passing Time. So Never let it go for silly fights or reasons.

Thank You So Much Message

For Your Supported & For Your Loves Thank You So Much. Have A Greatest Day Of Your. If I am successful today, because of my father, if he lived today, he would have been very happy, he will always and always be with me.